SHARKS

Chloe Schroeter

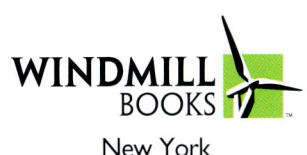

New York

Published in 2015 by Windmill Books, An Imprint of Rosen Publishing
29 East 21st Street, New York, NY 10010

Copyright © 2015 by Miles Kelly Publishing Ltd/Windmill Books, An Imprint of Rosen Publishing

All rights reserved. No part of this book may be reproduced in any form without permission in writing from the publisher, except by a reviewer.

US Editor: Joshua Shadowens
Publishing Director: Belinda Gallagher
Creative Director: Jo Cowan
Senior Editor: Rosie McGuire
Assistant Editor: Chlöe Schroeter
Volume Design: Sally Lace
Cover Designer: Jo Cowan
Indexer: Hilary Bird
Production Manager: Elizabeth Collins
Reprographics: Stephan Davis, Thom Allaway, Lorraine King

All artwork from the Miles Kelly Artwork Bank
Cover: R. Gino Santa Maria/Shutterstock.com

Library of Congress Cataloging-in-Publication Data

Schroeter, Chloe, author.
Sharks / by Chloe Schroeter.
    pages cm. — (Animal Q & A)
Includes index.
ISBN 978-1-4777-9198-1 (library binding) — ISBN 978-1-4777-9199-8 (pbk.) — ISBN 978-1-4777-9200-1 (6-pack)
1. Sharks—Miscellanea—Juvenile literature. 2. Children's questions and answers. I. Title.
QL638.9.S2925 2015
597.3—dc23
                                        2014001240

Manufactured in the United States of America

CPSIA Compliance Information: Batch #WS14WM: For Further Information contact Windmill Books, New York, New York at 1-866-478-0556

Contents

J
597.3
SCH

What is a shark?	4
Where in the world do sharks live?	4
How many types of shark are there?	5
How does a shark swim?	6
How does a shark breathe?	7
Do sharks have good senses?	7
Why do sharks have pointy teeth?	8
Do sharks go to sleep?	8
What do sharks eat?	9
Do sharks lay eggs?	10
Do sharks look after their babies?	11
What are baby sharks called?	11
Which shark can disappear?	12
How do sharks find mates?	13
Do sharks have cousins?	13
Which fish stick to sharks?	14
Do sharks have friends?	15
Do sharks lose their teeth?	15

Which shark is as big as a whale?	16
Which shark digs for its dinner?	17
Why are sharks so scary?	17
Can small sharks be fierce?	18
Do sharks use hammers?	19
Which shark is a big-mouth?	19
Can sharks be prickly?	20
When is a shark like a zebra?	21
Do sharks eat people?	21
Are all sharks dangerous?	22
Glossary	23
Further Reading	23
Index	24
Websites	24

What is a shark?

→ Blue shark

A shark is a meat-eating fish that lives in the sea. All sharks have a strong sense of smell to help them find their prey — the animals they hunt for food. Most sharks have a big mouth and sharp teeth.

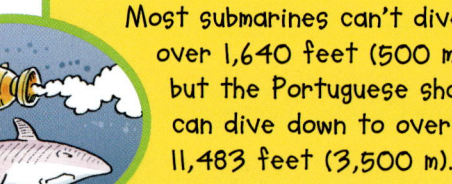
→ Whale shark

Shark submarines!
Most submarines can't dive over 1,640 feet (500 m), but the Portuguese shark can dive down to over 11,483 feet (3,500 m).

Where in the world do sharks live?

Sharks live in seas and oceans around the world. They are often found by the coast, a few miles (km) from the beach. Each type of shark has its own favorite place to live.

How many types of sharks are there?

There are around 350 kinds of sharks. The most common is the blue shark. Each type of shark is different in size, color and markings. Types of sharks can also behave differently.

Draw

Sketch a scary shark with big teeth chasing small fish in the sea.

How does a shark swim?

Sand tiger shark

A shark swims by using its fins. The tail itself is a fin, and moves from side to side using strong muscles to push the shark through the water. The fin on the top of the body is called the dorsal fin. This keeps the shark upright in the water.

Shark cookies!
The cookie-cutter shark was given its name because of how it feeds. It bites its prey and then swivels its sharp teeth in a circle to cut away a cookie-shaped lump of flesh.

How does a shark breathe?

A shark breathes through its gills, which are slits on the sides of its head. Most sharks have to keep swimming all the time so that water is always flowing over their gills, allowing them to breathe.

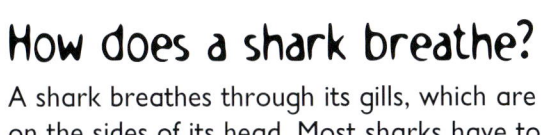
Dorsal fin

Gills

Play
Sharks have good night-time eyesight. When you next go to bed, see how well you can see in the dark.

Do sharks have good senses?

Yes! Sharks can see well even at night, and can smell blood from several miles (km) away. Hearing is not their best sense, but they can still hear scuba divers breathing. Their ears are tiny holes just behind their eyes.

Why do sharks have pointy teeth?

So they can saw lumps of flesh off the animals they catch! The teeth are narrow with sharp areas along their edges. The great white shark's teeth grow up to 2.4 inches (6 cm) in length – that's about the size of your middle finger.

Do sharks go to sleep?

Most sharks don't sleep. However, whale sharks sometimes stop swimming to rest on the seabed. They can stay still like this for months. This helps them save energy when there is not much food.

Sneaky shark!

The blind shark of Australia isn't blind at all! It has thick eyelids that when shut, make the shark look blind.

Tiger shark

What do sharks eat?

Sharks eat all kinds of meat, including fish and seals. Some sharks hunt and chase their prey, or feast on dying or dead animals. Other sharks lie in wait for food, and some swim open-mouthed to swallow small prey in the water.

Great white shark

Count

Whale sharks can stay still in the water for months. Time how long you can stay still for.

Do sharks lay eggs?

Some sharks do lay eggs, but others give birth to live babies. A shark egg contains the young shark and a yolk. The yolk feeds the shark until it hatches. An empty egg case is called a "mermaid's purse."

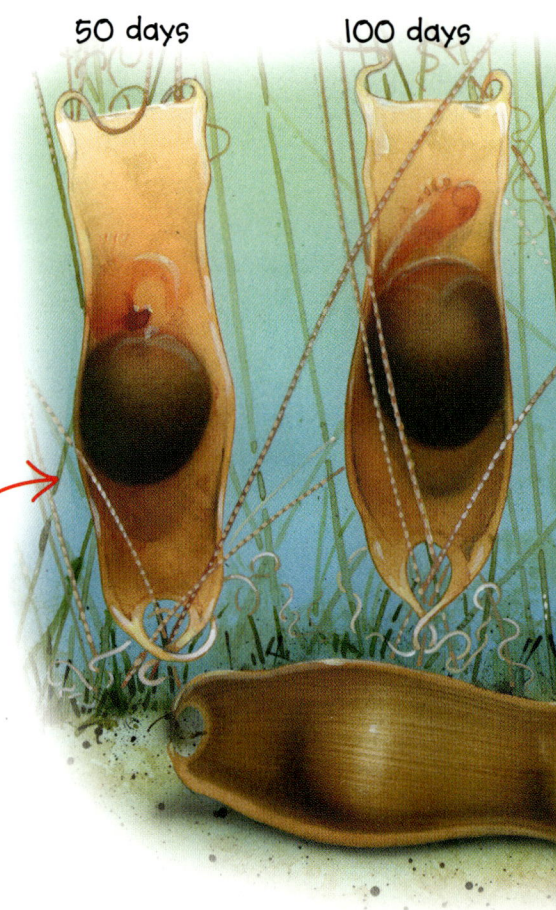

50 days   100 days

Egg

Think
Sharks are not the only animals that lay eggs. How many egg-laying animals can you think of?

Do sharks look after their babies?

No they don't. As soon as they are born, baby sharks have to look after themselves. They have to hunt for their own food and protect themselves against other creatures that try to eat them.

Hungry pups!

As the young of the sand tiger shark grow inside their mother, the biggest one with the most developed teeth may feed on the smaller, weaker ones.

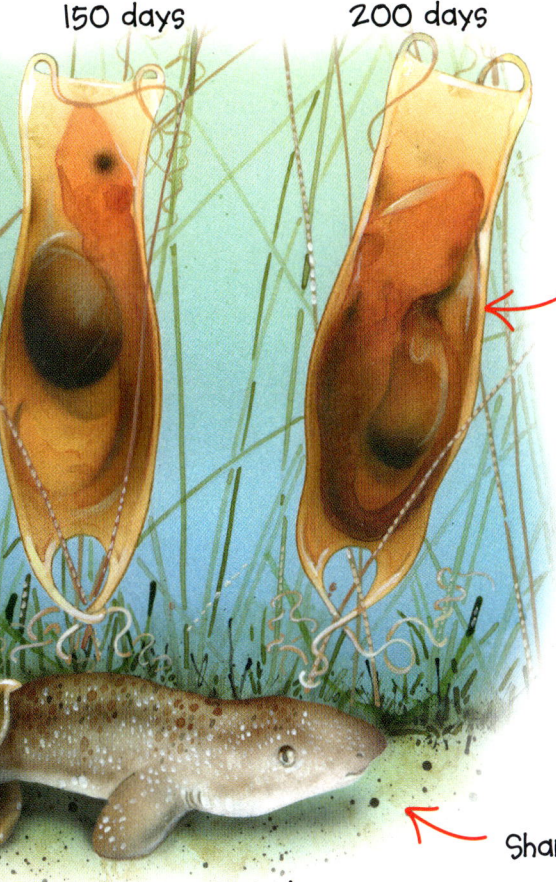

150 days

200 days

Pup developing in an egg

Shark pup

250 days

What are baby sharks called?

Baby sharks are called pups. They normally look like smaller versions of their parents, but have brighter colors and markings. Many pups get eaten, as they are easy prey for dolphins, sea lions and other sharks.

Which shark can disappear?

An angel shark can. Its wide, flat body is sand-colored so it blends perfectly with the seabed. These sharks are called angel sharks because their fins spread out wide like an angel's wings. They can lie in wait for over a week until the right food comes along.

Angel shark

Hide
See if you can blend into your surroundings like an angel shark. Can anyone find you?

How do sharks find mates?

They use their sense of smell! When it's time to make babies, sharks give off special smells into the water to attract one another. Some sharks don't mate very often, and can become rare.

← White-tip reef sharks

Do sharks have cousins?

Yes, they do – in a way. Sharks have close relations such as skates and rays. The bodies of these fish are similar to those of sharks. Stingrays have sharp spines on their tails. These contain poison that they stab into prey, or any creatures that try to attack them.

Greedy shark!

A dead greenland shark was once found with a whole reindeer in its stomach! These sharks usually eat fish and squid, but they have been known to eat dead whales.

Which fish stick to sharks?

Fish called sharksuckers do! Using a ridged sucker on their heads, they stick onto large sharks so they don't have to swim, and can go wherever the shark goes. When the shark finds a meal, the sharksucker can break off and steal what food is left.

Bull shark

Sharksucker

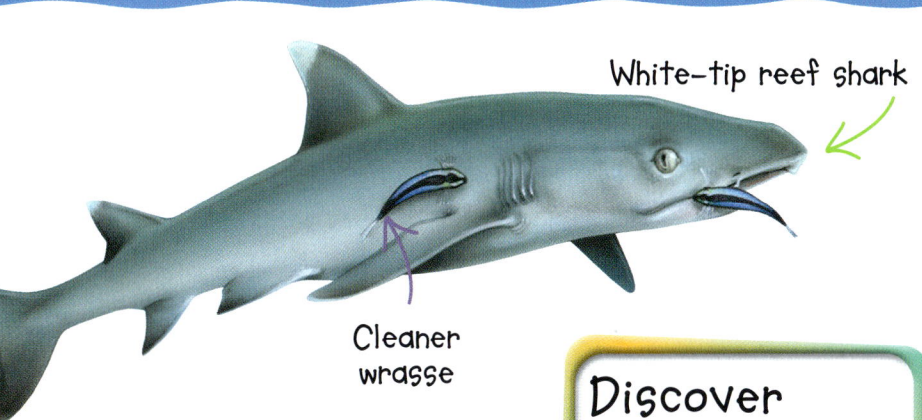

White-tip reef shark

Cleaner wrasse

Do sharks have friends?

Sharks and cleaner wrasse fish help each other. Sharks even let these fish into their mouths without eating them. The cleaner wrasse eat the dirt on the shark's teeth, and in return the shark gets its teeth cleaned.

Discover
Blue sharks swim across the Atlantic Ocean from the Caribbean to western Europe. Find these places on a map.

Glowing sharks!
Lanternsharks can glow in the dark. The light they create attracts small creatures such as fish and squid, so the shark can snap them up.

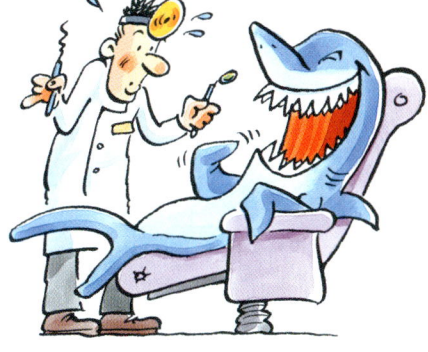

Do sharks lose their teeth?

Yes — most shark's teeth are quite narrow and can snap off. New teeth are always growing to replace any that are lost. Some sharks lose over 3,000 teeth in their lifetime.

Which shark is as big as a whale?

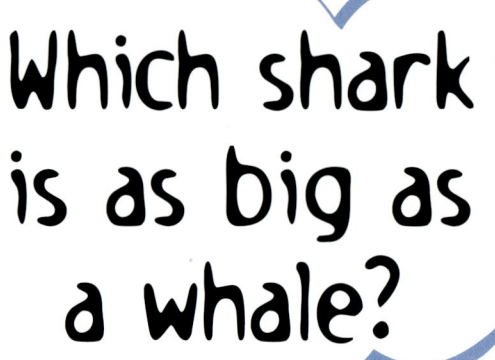

The whale shark is. In fact it is the biggest shark of all. It can grow to be as long as five cars – that's 66 feet (20 m) in length. Whale sharks can weigh more than 13.2 tons (12 t) – that's the same weight as 12 large horses.

Whale shark

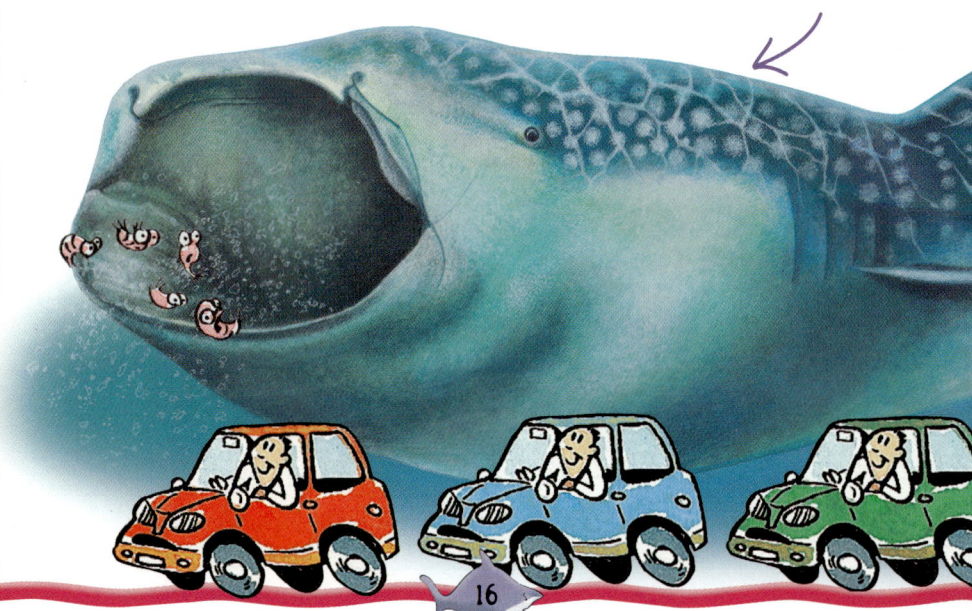

← Saw shark

Which shark digs for its dinner?

The saw shark does! Its long nose is surrounded by teeth, so it looks like a saw. They use their noses to dig up prey from the seabed. Then they slash and tear at the food.

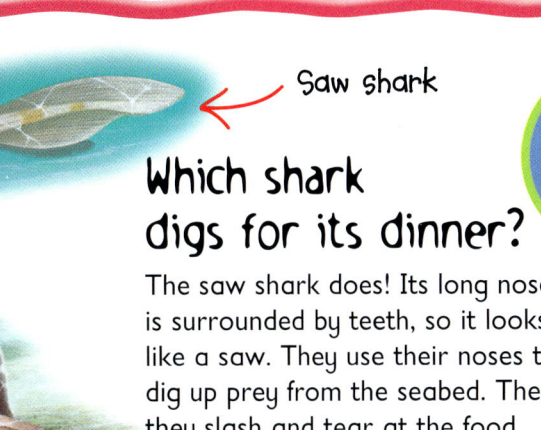

Dinner time!

Krill look like small shrimps and are up to 1.2 inches (3 cm) in length. Whale sharks feed by taking water into their mouths and trapping krill before swallowing them.

Find out

Use the Internet or books to find information and pictures about krill. Where do they live?

Why are sharks so scary?

Sharks seem scary because they are so big and have sharp teeth. We feel unable to protect ourselves against them. Sharks are often shown in films and on television as more dangerous than they really are.

17

Can small sharks be fierce?

They can when they hunt in a group. Pygmy sharks are one of the smallest types of shark, at only 7.1 to 7.9 inches (18–20 cm) in length. By working together they can attack and kill fish much larger than themselves. Luckily, pygmy sharks are harmless to humans.

Pygmy sharks

Think
If you had discovered the megamouth shark what would you have called it? What other shark names can you think of?

Do sharks use hammers?

A hammerhead does! Its hammer-shaped head gives it a better sense of smell. This is because its nostrils are far apart, one on each side of its head. This helps the hammerhead to find out quickly where a smell is coming from, so it can track down its food.

Megamouth shark

Tiny sharks!
The smallest sharks could lie curled up in your hand. The dwarf lanternshark is at most 8.3 inches (21 cm) in length.

Which shark is a big-mouth?

The megamouth shark's mouth is more than 4.3 feet (1.3 m) in width. Inside are rows of tiny teeth. This shark swims through schools of fish with its mouth wide open, trapping and swallowing its prey.

Can sharks be prickly?

Yes they can! Most sharks have tough, slightly spiky skin. The bramble shark is a deep-water shark that has very prickly skin. It is covered in large, sharp thorn-like spikes that act as protection from predators.

Bramble shark

Hot sharks!

Unlike most sharks, great whites are partly warm-blooded. This helps the muscles in their bodies work better, allowing them to swim quickly when hunting.

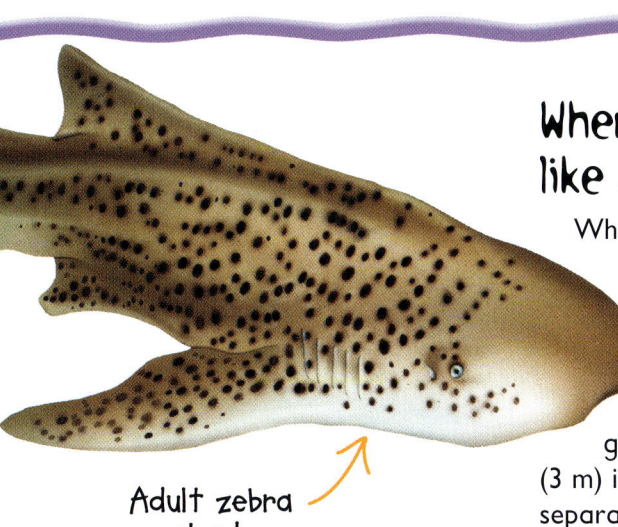

Adult zebra shark

When is a shark like a zebra?

When it is young, a zebra shark is covered in stripes. It has dark and pale stripes that run along its body. As it gets older it grows up to 9.8 feet (3 m) in length, and its stripes separate, turning into spots.

Draw
Design a poster to show why we need to look after sharks, and how people can help.

Do sharks eat people?

Sharks very rarely eat people. If they do attack, it's because they think we are prey, or because they are hungry. Most people survive shark attacks, because once sharks realize the person is not their usual food, they leave them alone.

Are all sharks dangerous?

No, most sharks are harmless. However some sharks such as the great white, tiger and bull shark have been known to attack people. These sharks are always on the look-out for food, which is why they can be dangerous.

A great white shark

Count
Now that you have read this book, how many different kinds of sharks can you remember?

Glossary

dangerous (DAYN-jeh-rus) Able to cause harm.
dorsal fin (DOR-sul-FIN) A fin on the back of a fish or water nomad.
gills (GILZ) Body parts that fish use for breathing.
krill (KRIL) Tiny sea animals.
mate (MAYT) To join together to make babies. Lower predators
prey (PRAY) An animal that is hunted by another animal for food.
pups (PUPs) A type of baby animals.
reindeer (RAYN-dir) Large deer that live in the Arctic.
seabed (SEE-bed) The floor of the sea or ocean.
spikes (SPYKS) Sharp, pointy things shaped like a spear or a needle.
submarines (SUB-muh-reenz) Ships that are made to travel underwater.
wrasse (RAS) A very large and diverse family of fish with a variety of uses.

Further Reading

Niver, Heather Moore. *20 Fun Facts About Sharks*. Fun Fact File: Animals! New York: Gareth Stevens, 2012.
Owen, Ruth. *Great White Shark*. Real Life Sea Monsters. New York: PowerKids Press, 2014.
Royston, Angela. *Shark: Killer King of the Ocean*. Top of the Food Chain. New York: Windmill Books, 2014.

Index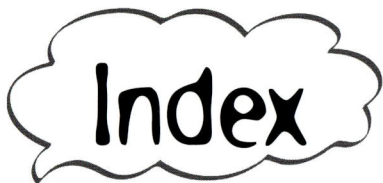

A
angel shark 10
babies, 10, 13
beach, 4
blood, 7

C
cars, 16
coast, 4
color(s), 5, 11

D
dirt, 15
dolphins, 11

E
egg(s), 10
energy, 8
eyes, 7

F
films, 17
fin(s), 6, 12

G
gills, 7

H
horses, 16

K
krill, 17

M
markings, 5, 11
mouth(s), 4, 15, 17, 19
muscles, 6, 20

N
nostrils, 19

O
oceans, 4

B
people, 21–22
poison, 13

prey, 4, 6, 9, 11, 13, 17, 19, 21
pups, 11

R
rays, 13

S
sea(s), 4
seabed, 8, 12, 17
seals, 9
spots, 21

T
teeth, 4, 6, 8, 15, 17, 19
television, 17

W
world, 4
wrasse, 15

Y
yolk, 10

Websites

For web resources related to the subject of this book, go to: www.windmillbooks.com/weblinks and select this book's title.